CW00872081

THE URBAN TURBANS

DAHLIAN KIRBY

Illustrated by
Adam Fisher

Pont

For my big sister Carole

Published in 2007 by Pont Books, an imprint of
Gomer Press, Llandysul, Ceredigion, SA44 4JL

ISBN 978 1 84323 807 2

A CIP record for this title is available from the British Library.

This book is published with the financial support of the
Welsh Books Council.

Printed and bound in Wales at
Gomer Press, Llandysul, Ceredigion

Chapter 1

Music! Music in every room in the house! It was awful! It was terrible. There was no escape!

Megan's family was musical – there was no doubt about it. There was always some music playing somewhere, either the radio or a CD or someone with a musical instrument, practising. Practising was the worst, the same old bit of noise playing over and over again.

Dad was a music teacher and a composer. Sometimes he taught people at home. Why anybody would want to do extra work after school, Megan didn't understand. When Dad was being a composer, his hair stood on end and he played the piano way too loud and said things like *Magnificent*! and *I'm nearly there*! He always shouted a lot when he was composing.

Mum played the violin in an orchestra. She had to wear long black skirts which she sometimes tripped over. Her violin was worth lots of money and was called Doris. Megan hated the sounds Doris made. Yes, she knew that Mum was a great star in the orchestra and that people adored her.

But, to Megan, violin music sounded very, very bad. And that was just the start.

Megan's big brother, Martyn, played the piano (nasty!), her big sisters, Catrin and Carys, both played the harp (terrible!) and her little brother, Gari, played the recorder (pathetic!). Gari had asked for a trumpet for Christmas. It was enough to make Megan want to leave home! A trumpet for Christmas? He was only six years old. Megan thought he should be playing with toys not trumpets.

She hated all this music, all the noise of it, all the bits of paper with squiggles on telling you what to play. What Megan liked was action! She liked climbing trees and riding horses and swimming in the sea and running through the fields with her dog, Daisy.

So when Mum and Dad decided to move to a house in the big city, Megan was not at all happy. OK, it was a big house; OK, it was still near the sea; OK, there were lots of good places to visit. OK, it had two bathrooms and Megan would have a much bigger bedroom. But . . . it had a tiny garden; there were no horses for miles; it wasn't 'real' sea where you could paddle or swim; and the trees looked so skinny that Megan thought they would snap if you tried to climb them. It was all right for everyone else because they had music. They just stayed in making music and telling each other how wonderful they sounded. Yuck!

On the other hand, Megan quite enjoyed her new school and the other children were very friendly. Their families came from all over the world, which was very interesting for someone who was just used to people who came from Wales. It was great too that none of the other parents was a musician and none of her friends seemed to play a musical instrument.

After school Megan would go home with her new friends Jamila and Luke, and they would do things like watching cartoons or going on the play-station. It was wonderful; it was heaven; it was not music! Suddenly, moving to the city didn't seem such a bad thing.

Sometimes Megan and her new friends went to the park or went swimming at the local pool. Sometimes they went bowling with Luke's mum and stepdad. Megan loved bowling. She loved the feel of the ball. She loved the burgers and chips they ate in the cafè afterwards. She loved everything about the place.

Sometimes the friends went to the cinema or had take-away meals. Jamila's big brother delivered food for a Chinese take-away and his boss sometimes allowed him to bring some home. The food was wonderful, all soft and tasty. It came in little metal boxes and Jamila and Megan liked to eat it with chopsticks. Sometimes the food fell off the chopsticks and onto the sofa – Jamila's mum didn't seem to mind, as long as it was all cleaned up before Megan went home.

At weekends, sometimes, Mum and Dad took Megan and her little brother to the seafront, about half an hour's ride away. Sometimes they went to the big park in the middle of the city. The beach was good, but it had a concrete promenade and shops; the park was OK, but it wasn't like the real countryside. It was too crowded.

Megan missed the countryside; she missed horse riding. But she loved eating Chinese food with chopsticks and her bowling was coming on really well.

Then it happened. The thing that Megan was dreading.

Chapter 2

'We have some special guests with us today,' said Mrs Evans, Megan's head teacher. It was the beginning of assembly. She smiled as if something wonderful was about to happen. Megan stopped talking to Jamila and waited to see who the special guests were.

She got a nasty surprise when onto the stage walked four grown-ups, all carrying musical instruments. There was a man with a flute, another man with a keyboard and two women, one carrying a collection of recorders and the other carrying a trumpet.

'Welcome!' boomed Mrs Evans. 'These are our special guests; they have come from the county music service and as you can see, they have brought their instruments with them. Now, can anybody tell me what the instruments are called?'

About fifty hands shot up, eager children all wanting to tell Mrs Evans what they knew. Megan kept her hands down.

This was so boring! It took about ten minutes

for children to guess the right answers. Lots of people thought that the trumpet was a saxophone and that the recorders were flutes. The worst bit was when the recorder woman wanted the children to tell her exactly which kind of recorder she was holding up. Nobody knew. Well, Megan did. But she wasn't saying a word. She had known since she was about two years old.

At last even the lady with the recorders got fed up of waiting. 'This is the tenor recorder, this is the descant recorder, and this one is the treble recorder,' she said.

Mrs Evans smiled again. Megan didn't know what there was to smile about. She knew that any minute now, those musicians were going to play their boring old instruments.

'Well, children,' said Mrs Evans, 'David, Steve, Helen and Lucy are all going to play you a tune, just to show you what their instruments can do. After assembly, anyone who wants to learn to play an instrument must wait behind.'

Back in the classroom Mrs Williams thanked her children for sitting so quietly in assembly. Then she said, 'Doesn't anyone want to learn a musical instrument?' She seemed surprised that no-one had stayed behind. There was silence. Megan could feel herself blushing.

Luke poked her in the side and whispered, 'You can play a musical instrument, can't you?'

Megan shook her head.

'Megan,' said Mrs Williams, 'you come from a musical family. Surely you must play something?' Megan shook her head. 'I thought your mum told me you can play the flute.'

'No, miss, I can't,' fibbed Megan. She hated the flute. Nasty cold bit of metal.

'Well!' said Mrs Williams. 'We are very lucky that our school has been chosen. You don't have to own an instrument, you know: your parents can borrow one. It doesn't matter if you didn't stay behind in the hall because I have some letters here to give out to anyone who would like to learn to play an instrument. It is a great opportunity. As you know, Wales is the land of song. We are very proud of our music. So, who would like to take a letter home?'

Megan sat on her hands, just to make sure one didn't shoot up by accident. Almost half the class wanted to learn. Mrs Williams gave them all letters.

After school Megan was going straight to Jamila's house. The two girls walked home with Luke who lived two doors away. As soon as they had left the playground, Luke said to Megan, 'You told a fib to Mrs Williams.'

Megan stood still. She looked at Luke and blushed. She had very pale skin and when she blushed, it was spectacular. She could feel her face and head going all red. Knowing it was happening made her feel worse, which made her blush an even deeper red.

'You can play a musical instrument,' said Luke.

'She can play three,' said Jamila. 'Her mum told me. She can play the piano, the flute and the recorder. Why did you lie, Megan?'

Megan looked at her two friends. She felt like running away. She really didn't want to go home with Jamila now. She started to cry.

'It doesn't matter,' said Jamila.

'Why did you fib, Megan?' asked Luke in a kind voice. 'You are a nice person . . . Did you have to fib? Why did you have to?'

They had reached Jamila's front door. Megan took out a tissue and wiped her eyes. 'Everyone in my family is mad about music. Everyone but me. I like excitement and adventure. If you play an instrument, you have to sit still and play what it says on the sheet. You have to do as you are told. I get enough of that in class. I want to enjoy myself . . . not sit still and play boring old music.'

At about six o'clock Jamila's brother turned up with some Chinese food. Everybody tucked into chicken and sweetcorn with egg fried rice. It was delicious.

'Do you want the good news or the bad news?' asked Jamila's brother.

'The bad,' said Jamila, trying to hold a piece of sweetcorn between her chopsticks.

'This is my last day in this job. So no more free Chinese take-aways.'

'What's the good news?' Megan wanted to know.

'I start working for the Indian take-away next week!'

Megan had never had Indian food: she didn't know if she'd like it. It would be a bit embarrassing if she didn't. 'What's Indian food like?' she asked Jamila.

'Spicy. Lots of rice. Do you want to watch a DVD?'

They settled down with milk shakes to watch a film. It was great being at Jamila's. Megan had forgotten all about the musicians at school. Forgotten about the fib to her teacher.

Chapter 3

It was a lovely warm day, quite hot for April. Everybody – Mum, Dad, Martyn, Catrin, Carys, Megan and Gari – had come to the park for the big spring celebration. There was to be a bouncy castle, stalls and a small fair. At least it's not music, thought Megan.

The park was in the grounds of a beautiful castle, which looked like something out of a fairy tale. Megan thought it must be very old but her dad said that it wasn't. There were lots of people in the park, but it was so big that it didn't seem crowded.

First, Megan and Gari went on the bouncy castle. Next everybody – even Martyn, who usually thought he was too grown-up for such things – went on the dodgem cars. After that they had a look at some of the stalls. Megan and Mum spent a while looking at the herbs and plants whilst everybody else went to look at the books. There were lots of food stalls too. Mum and Dad bought some Welsh cheese and some home-made chocolates.

At lunchtime everyone drifted away from the stalls and sat down under a massive tree. As it was such a lovely day, Mum had brought a picnic. The food was very nice, all the stuff Megan used to like when she was little. There were egg sandwiches and sausage rolls and chicken drumsticks. But it wasn't quite as nice as the food Megan had at Jamila's house: now she liked samosas best.

After they had eaten, Dad, Martyn and Gari played football and Carys and Catrin went back for another look at the book stalls. Mum settled herself against the tree to read a book called *Restringing Your Violin*. How boring, thought Megan.

Ten minutes later Megan felt double bored. Another five, and she was mega-mega-totally-the-worst-ever bored. 'I'm going for a walk,' she said.

'That's nice,' said Mum. 'Don't go far and don't talk to strangers.'

Megan walked along until she came to a small wood. There were a few people lying on the grass or playing but nobody looked up as Megan walked past. The wood was lovely with lots of different trees. She knew the names of some of them, the easy ones like the horse chestnuts

which had already started to put out their candle
flowers. Then she heard a sound in the distance.
A truly magical sound. It made her feel scared
and happy all at the same time.

It was happening on the other side of the wood. The sound came again. Another one, like the first, but different. It didn't sound like an animal; it didn't really sound like a person. It was *almost* like thunder; it was *almost* like a waterfall.

Megan walked slowly through the wood towards the magical, magnificent noise. There were now five different sounds. They were like each other, but not quite the same.

Megan was not afraid, not afraid of the wood or the sounds. She knew her mum was near, but she didn't really need her. She just had to see what was happening. Soon she was stepping out from the trees on the other side of the wood.

There were five young-looking men standing facing her. They all had a huge drum hanging on a thick cord from their necks. They all wore turbans. They were hitting the drums and were so busy thinking about what looked like a last-minute practice that they didn't notice Megan.

She didn't want to frighten them or put them off their drumming so she turned and went back into the wood. There were other children and parents around. Why weren't they listening to this amazing sound?

Megan sat down on a log and listened. Drums?

Well they looked like drums but the sound was like nothing she had ever heard before.

Someone was calling. Someone was calling her name. It was Mum and she sounded cross. Oops! Megan got up from the log and ran back through the wood. Mum told her off for going off so far on her own but Megan didn't listen. She just tapped her fingers against her leg, remembering the drums.

It was just impossible. She had been trying to make a drum for several days now. She had used paper, cardboard, leather and an old biscuit tin. She tried again with the bread bin until Dad told her off for messing up the kitchen, just when Megan thought she had almost got the right sound. If she put two blankets on the table and hit it with a wooden coat hanger, she could get a sound which was almost like one of the drums.

'Stop that stupid noise!' shouted her big brother.

'Why don't you go and play with your friends?' suggested Mum.

'That's a rubbish musical instrument,' said Gari.

Musical instrument? She didn't want a musical instrument. She wanted a magic drum, the same as the boys in the park. Megan tidied away the blankets and coat hanger. She was going to be late for tea at Jamila's if she didn't hurry.

She was late! Megan thought for a moment then decided to go down the shortcut lane. It ran from her street to the street before Jamila's house. She didn't usually go that way because people dumped rubbish down there and she didn't like it.

As she was walking along the lane, keeping to one side to avoid the bin bags and boxes of junk, she thought she heard something. Not the usual sort of something, like traffic noise or a radio playing in the distance. A different kind of something. A sound but more than a sound – like fireworks or the roaring of a lion. It sounded happy but fierce all at the same time. Bang boom! Bang boom! Faster and louder, until Megan thought that maybe the sky would come crashing down. But it didn't and after a minute the drums stopped.

Were they drums? They sounded the same but somehow not quite the same. Why would those magic drums be playing down this smelly, messy lane? Then they started again, quietly at first, then louder and faster. Megan ran towards them, as if magic was pulling her forward to the end of the lane and round the corner into the street before

Jamila's. The last but one house wasn't a house at all: it looked more like an old school. The bricks were dirty and the windows were dark, but there was no doubt that this was where the drumming was coming from. Bravely Megan approached the building, stood on tiptoe and looked in through one of the grimy downstairs windows.

What a sight to behold! Through the glass Megan could see the drummers, the same men that she had seen in the park. She had a closer view of the drums now. They were all different sizes and were hung on thick ribbons around the men's necks. And they were boys really, not men. High school boys. They all wore brightly-coloured turbans. The boys were smiling and sort of marching on the spot.

In one corner of the room there stood an old man with a long grey beard. The man was urging the boys to play louder and faster. It was the most exciting thing that Megan could ever remember. She wanted to go into that room and take one of the drums and beat it and march and smile the way the boys were smiling.

She knew that she couldn't. Why not? Well, she didn't really know. For one thing, she was only eleven; for another, she was a girl – and they were all boys. Megan waited till they had finished playing then ran all the way to Jamila's house. She didn't tell Jamila about the drums. She didn't want to talk about it.

Megan soon managed to find out when the drummers had their practice sessions. They practised every Tuesday from four until five and sometimes they practised on Fridays too. Megan would position herself outside the building and listen to them. If she put her back against the wall, she could feel her whole body shake from the power of the drums. It was the best thing in her entire life.

It took two whole months for Megan to work out a plan. Even now she wasn't totally sure it would work. She had been desperate to play a drum since she had first seen the boys practising in the youth club. She'd been right that it had once been a school. It only became a youth club when the new school was built.

During their Friday practices the boys would take a break. They left the drums and went into another room to play pool. Megan would stare though the window at the drums, left all alone. If only she could pluck up the courage to walk through the door of the youth club and go into that room.

One particular Friday, Megan arrived early. She could no longer be patient. Besides, she'd had a really dull day at school. Jamila had gone to her auntie's house for the evening and Luke had gone out with his brother. Megan's family had plans to spend the evening watching some stupid opera DVD so she would be all alone. It was like a sign. Tonight was the night.

She waited until the drummers had gone for their break, then took a very deep breath and boldly walked through the youth club door. She found herself in a wide entrance hall. The walls were full of glass cases – trophies and old black and white photos of men in long shorts wearing boxing gloves. Right in front of her there was a large glass case with an old wooden pole in it. There was a notice which said:

Grangetown – the beginning of baseball.

Not waiting to wonder what the wooden pole could be, Megan went straight to the first door on the right. There they were. Five beautiful drums, all alone. Megan could hear sounds in the distance: people talking, a pool ball being hit. Someone laughed. It all seemed so far away. Megan felt safe in the room with only the drums.

She walked over to the smallest one, paused for half a second then lifted it up and hung it round her neck.

Megan had planned to beat the drum softly, just to get a feel of it, just to know that she could. She would beat the drum for three minutes, she decided. She started as she meant to, listening to the dull thud. Then she played a little louder and just a little louder.

And if she hadn't been playing quite so loudly, she might have sensed that the Urban Turbans, the classiest drum band in Wales, had stopped what they were doing. Someone was playing one of their drums! They ran from the pool room as quickly as they could.

Their teacher, Mr Singh, got to the room first. He flung the door open, ready to confront the rogue who had dared to touch one of his precious drums. What did he see when he entered the room? Just a girl – no older than nine or ten, he thought, long brown hair done up in a ponytail, just like his two granddaughters – swaying and playing Desraj's drum.

Desraj was next through the door. He was about to storm in but Mr Singh put a hand on his arm to stop him. 'She's doing no harm,' said the old man quietly.

The drum grew louder and louder; Megan swayed to the rhythm. It was as if the drum played her: it was in control. Then she opened her eyes and saw, to her horror, that she was being stared at by five drummers and their teacher. At once she started to cry.

The boys and Mr Singh came right into the room. Before they could say anything, Megan ran past them and out of the door. She ran as fast as she could, taking the shortcut, not caring that she was running through rubbish in the smelly lane.

Megan ran up to her room and shut her bedroom door. She didn't think they had followed her. She sat on her bed to get her breath back. The old man must have been angry. The drummers must hate her. How had she dared to touch their precious drums? She knew she would never be able to go back to the room, never be able to touch that drum again.

Chapter 4

In Megan's old school they had celebrated Harvest Festival, Christmas and Easter. In her new school, with children from so many different countries, they celebrated many different festivals. Two weeks ago they had celebrated Harvest and they had collected food to give to poor people. The vicar had come to talk to them. Her name was Caryl and she lived next door to Jamila. She didn't look like a vicar, but Jamila said that she was.

This Friday they were having a Divali assembly. The assembly was going to be really special. There were lots of songs and poems and some Indian dancing. There was going to be a short mime of the story of Rama and Sita.

The costumes were fantastic. Luke's mum had helped make some of them. Jamila, who was playing Sita, was going to wear a red and white sari. The boy playing Rama was dressed in a gold and purple outfit. Megan's favourite costume was the one belonging to Ravan, the king of the demons. It was red and black and he had an enormous ten-headed mask. Even though she knew it was just a mask, Megan found it scary – and exciting at the same time.

Some big children were coming from the High School to perform too and soon the hall was full of people.

Megan was playing the part of a deer. It was an easy part; best of all she didn't have to sing or play a musical instrument or dance. She just had to run around the stage wearing a deer mask while a CD of Indian music was being played. She thought it was a sad story, the enchanted deer tempting Rama away from his brother and wife.

Megan hadn't told her parents about the assembly, so they hadn't come. Megan didn't like the fuss they would have made. After all she was only going to be on stage for about a minute.

After the dancing and the poems and the songs, Megan's class performed the mime and Jamila did really well as Sita. Megan had to admit that the music wasn't so terrible; some bits were OK. She put on her mask and moved about the stage, pretending to be a deer, then skipped back to her class to take off her costume.

As she turned the corner, she saw her teacher, Mrs Williams, talking to someone. It was the old man, Mr Singh, from the youth club. Megan felt her hands begin to shake, and her legs felt all wobbly. He had obviously come to complain about her. Megan was terrified. Would she be thrown out of the school? What would her parents say?

She turned and ran back towards the hall. As she was passing the hall door, it opened and Mr Pritchard, the caretaker, came out. He held the door open for Megan, still in her mask and costume, to go in. She didn't know what to do for a moment. Then she thought perhaps it would be a good idea to go in and watch the performance. Some High School girls were doing an Indian dance. They got all the steps right and smiled all the way through the dance. Megan couldn't imagine ever looking that confident in front of people. Maybe it was because they were really old.

The old man in the turban came through the door and climbed the steps up to the stage. He waited until everyone had stopped talking and then he said, 'That was fantastic, wasn't it? And now we have something else to entertain you with. The boys who are about to perform are all ex-pupils of this school. Ladies and gentlemen, boys and girls: the Urban Turbans!'

Megan turned round. She had to get out of the

hall quickly, but there were now lots of people standing behind her and she couldn't get through. Then she realised that the people standing behind her were the drummers, waiting to get on stage. She moved out of their way but they didn't seem to have noticed her; they just hurried past; they couldn't wait to start playing.

The caretaker was now standing inside the door, leaning against it. There was no way out! Megan spun round, in total panic. Then the first boy shouted, 'One and two and . . .' and the drums began to play.

When their sound filled the school hall, some of the pupils and parents gasped in amazement. Nobody spoke or moved. The boys beat the drums harder and harder. They seemed tireless.

Megan sat down on a chair. She just watched and listened at first. Then she looked around her. Every single person seemed to be in the power of the drums. After twenty minutes the drummers slowed and stopped. Then the audience clapped and clapped while the performers bowed low and smiled. They didn't even look tired.

Megan didn't care if she looked silly in her deer mask. She couldn't take it off in case the drummers recognised her. Then a voice behind her said, 'Megan, we need some help with the cake stall.' It was Mrs Williams, her teacher. In the Infant Hall, drinks and food were being served to the parents and guests. Megan had said that she would help with the cakes but in her confusion she had completely forgotten.

Mrs Williams was smiling at her. Megan followed her down to the Infant Hall where there were stalls and a sort of café. There were fairy lights on the walls and there was Indian music playing. As Megan took up her place next to Luke on the cake stall, her hands were shaking. Could she get away with keeping the deer mask on?

'Are you going to wear that all day?' Luke asked. 'You look silly.'

'I think I will,' said Megan.

After fifteen minutes of selling cakes, she began to feel better. The man and the drummers had probably gone home by now. She was still worried about Mrs Williams finding out. But being told off by the drum teacher and the drummers would have been much, much worse.

Mr Singh entered the Infant Hall with the caretaker. 'I am in desperate need of a cup of tea.'

'You must be,' said Mr Pritchard. 'You work very hard with those drummers.'

'Oh, my boys are very good. I just need lots of tea to keep me going,' said Mr Singh, smiling.

'The tea stall is just over here,' said Mr Pritchard. 'I'll show you.'

'I would have got here sooner,' said Mr Singh, 'but so many people wanted to tell me how great the drums sounded. I am very proud of the boys. Proud but thirsty.'

The two men collected their cups of tea and sat down. Megan didn't know what to do. Then to make things worse, Luke decided to pull her mask off, as a joke. She usually loved his jokes, but not this time. He hid the mask behind his back.

'Give it back!' hissed Megan.

Mr Singh finished his tea and came over to the cake stall. 'Hello,' he said.

Megan blushed but she managed to say hello.

'Which cakes are the best ones do you think?' Mr Singh asked.

'The chocolate cornflake ones,' said Megan.

'Five of those then, please.' Mr Singh paused and smiled at her. 'Oh, and by the way, I run drum classes for juniors on Saturday mornings. At the Riverside Centre.' He reached into his pocket and brought out a leaflet. 'You will need to ask your parents if you can come.'

Then Mr Singh picked up his packet of chocolate cornflake cakes and left.

'Who was that?' Luke wanted to know.

Megan smiled and said, 'My new drum teacher.'

Megan couldn't wait for school to finish. She couldn't wait to show her mum and dad the leaflet about drum lessons. But . . . what if they said no? What if they wouldn't let her go? She had to learn the drums. She really did.

As it turned out, Megan's parents were thrilled. They thought it was wonderful that she wanted to learn a new musical instrument. 'You can start with this,' said Mum as she signed the form, 'and then maybe you can go back to your other instruments later.'

Hmm, thought Megan.

Chapter 5

Megan wanted to walk to her first drum lesson but Dad insisted on taking her in the car. Mr Singh had said that she could borrow one of his drums for a few weeks, just to see if she really liked playing. Really liked playing? Megan couldn't wait. She had to sit on her hands for the ten minutes' drive because she couldn't keep them still.

The drum lessons took place not in the youth club but in a church hall that smelled of old wallpaper and dust. Megan tried to say goodbye to Dad in the car but he followed her in, saying that he wanted to meet Mr Singh. So now her dad was talking to Mr Singh while she stood by a big table upon which lay several drums.

Megan breathed deeply, wanting to breathe the smell of the drums. And . . . they did smell! Of something sweet and warm. Maybe that was how India smelled.

The other children started to arrive. It looked like Megan would be the only child whose family wasn't from India. She hadn't thought about that.

They were Indian drums; playing them was called Indian drumming. Maybe she shouldn't be here . . .

She felt a bit better when a tall boy with bright orange hair came in through the door. He smiled at Megan then made for the table where the drums lay. He picked one up.

Megan's dad came and kissed her goodbye; then he was gone. There she was in the big dusty church hall with a lot of people she didn't know and an amazing collection of drums.

The lesson seemed to pass in moments. When Jamila asked her about it later that afternoon, Megan couldn't really describe it. 'We played. I played . . . I played a magic drum,' said Megan softly, the memory of the smell of sweetness and warmth tickling her nostrils.

'Yeah, OK,' said Jamila. 'But, you know, was it hard? Did you feel stupid because you were new? What did you learn?'

'I played the drum,' said Megan.

'Was it fun?' her best friend wanted to know.

'Yes. No. Well not fun. Magical. An amazing experience.'

'Good,' said Jamila. 'Now shall we go and call for Luke or do you want to stay in and have a go on the play-station?'

Every Saturday morning Megan set off to the church hall for her drum lesson. She had managed to persuade Dad not to take her, just to pick her up afterwards. 'I want to discuss your progress with Mr Singh,' he had explained.

The walk along the riverbank was part of the magic. Megan felt little flutters in her tummy that grew stronger the nearer she got to the church hall. She was always the first to arrive. After the third week Mr Singh started bringing an extra cup so that she could share some of the tea from his flask.

'I cannot think without tea,' Mr Singh would say as he poured the thick warm liquid into the two little metal cups. The tea smelled like the drums. The drums and the tea were part of the same thing. Something warm and sweet and magical.

'How's Megan doing?' asked her dad every week.

Mr Singh would smile and say, 'Magically. She has taken to it like nobody else. She is wonderful.'

Megan didn't like these little chats between Dad and Mr Singh. It wasn't her that was wonderful, but the drum. The drum did the work; she just followed Mr Singh's very easy instructions.

After six weeks Megan was promoted to the

afternoon class. She was the only pupil in the class still in primary school. There was one other Welsh girl, but she left after two weeks because she was moving to another town.

Megan started to take the drum home, so that she could practise. Her big sisters laughed at her. 'A drummer,' said Carys. 'Fancy having a drummer in the family!'

'Drums aren't real instruments,' said Catrin as she played her harp. 'Drummers aren't really musicians.'

Both of Megan's brothers complained that she played far too loudly. Her mum, who was proud of her daughter's drumming, had a different complaint. 'Megan, cariad,' she said one day. 'Keep still!'

Megan stopped drumming, opened her eyes and looked at her mum. She hadn't even heard her come into the bedroom.

'Can't you just sit down and play that thing?' Mum asked. 'Why do you have to move around so much?'

'I didn't know I was,' said Megan.

'Megan, you have been marching around your bedroom for half an hour, banging on that thing. We all thought you were going to come through the ceiling!'

Megan told Jamila and Luke what her mum had said. Jamila laughed.

'What's so funny?' asked Megan.

'You not knowing you were moving around,' said Jamila.

'You must have looked really silly,' said Luke.

Megan decided that she wouldn't talk about drumming with her friends. They were really nice people but they just didn't understand.

Sometimes the Urban Turbans themselves would come to watch the Saturday afternoon drum lessons. They had their lesson after Megan's group. 'Drums One' was the morning group. Megan was in 'Drums Two'. The Urban Turbans should have been called 'Drums Three', because they had worked their way up from Drums One and Two. They were, though, just called the Urban Turbans. They were a proper band. Megan wondered why they needed lessons when they were so obviously brilliant at drumming.

One Saturday Megan asked one of them, whose name was Jagraj, why he had drum lessons when he was so good. Jagraj laughed and said, 'There is always something new to learn.'

Mostly the Turbans said nice things about the people in the other classes. Sometimes they asked if they could join in, as if they were the junior players! Megan loved it when this happened. The Urban Turbans would put their drums round their necks and they would begin to play. When the Urban Turbans joined in, everything was faster and louder and Megan had to work very hard to keep up.

On the day she talked to Jagraj, Mr Singh suggested that Megan and a boy called Shiva should play along with the Urban Turbans whilst the other children watched and listened.

Megan couldn't believe she had been chosen! She knew that Shiva was a really good drummer and that he hoped to join the Turbans one day. She hoped she could be good enough too. She stroked the drum softly with her fingers and whispered, 'Come on, Mr Dhol. Help me.' She called her borrowed drum Mr Dhol because it was a dhol drum. She loved the word 'dhol' and had learned to say it the way Indian people did.

The Urban Turbans started, and then Mr Singh counted in Shiva and Megan. She waited for the signal, and began to play. Faster and faster, louder and louder. It was all over in a few minutes but it had been amazing. The Urban Turbans had helped them play better than either could have imagined. They knew they had made a few mistakes, but they felt very pleased with themselves.

While Megan was waiting for Dad to ask the usual questions about her progress, she listened to the Turbans talking about a show they were going to perform that night.

Jagraj looked at her and said, 'You should come tonight. Shiva is coming with his parents. You never know; one day you might play with us for an audience.'

Megan felt herself blush, a happiness sort of blush. As she walked past Desraj, though, he sneered at her. Then he said, 'Jagraj was just being kind to you. Don't ever think you could play with us on stage. You're not that good, right? Anyway, you're just a kid; you aren't even Indian.' Then he laughed in a gruff sort of way and added, 'Besides you couldn't exactly wear a turban, could you?'

In the car, after her lesson, Dad said that Mr Singh had given them free tickets to go and see the performance.

'I don't want to go,' said Megan.

'Why not?' asked her dad. 'I thought you loved Indian drumming.'

'I do,' said Megan. 'I just don't want to go.'

The next Saturday Mr Singh handed Megan a

cup of hot, sweet tea then he said, 'I am sorry that you and your parents couldn't come to see the Turbans play last week. But, there will be another performance at my niece's wedding tomorrow. Would you like to come?'

Of course she wanted to. Her favourite band in the world playing her favourite music. Probably lots of nice Indian food. But no. She wasn't Indian. She wouldn't know what to wear or what to say. So she said, 'No thanks, I think we are doing something tomorrow.'

Only two of the Urban Turbans came to the practice that day: Jagraj, who always had a smile for everyone, and his cousin Desraj, who laughed in a way that sounded like he wasn't happy.

Jagraj led the session, while Mr Singh sat in his chair and had another cup of tea. Shiva was away on holiday in India, so Jagraj asked Megan to be the lead drummer. She was about to say that she wasn't good enough when Mr Singh shouted across the hall, 'Good idea! About time! Show us what you are made of, Megan!'

It was a great afternoon. Afterwards Mr Singh suggested to Megan's dad that it might be a good idea for her to watch the Urban Turbans rehearsing. 'That way, she would be getting free lessons. I believe you live near the youth club.'

He then turned to Megan and said, 'Call in any Friday. You are always most welcome.'

Megan waited near the door while Dad asked Mr Singh the usual questions. Again Desraj laughed at her. 'You think you are a great Indian drummer. You are just a spoilt little girl! Come and watch us if you want to. But that's all you're good for. Watching, not playing.'

Megan went all hot and then all cold. Her tummy jumped. Desraj laughed then walked away to talk to Jagraj.

I can't believe that they are cousins, thought Megan. Jagraj, well he wasn't exactly fat but he wasn't exactly skinny either. He had a big round face that reminded Megan of the full moon. He was always laughing and never said a bad word about any one. Desraj was much shorter and thinner. He laughed but he was never happy. You are just a bully, thought Megan.

Desraj had almost put Megan off going to the Urban Turbans' rehearsals. But . . . to be there would be wonderful. She would pick up tips and learn lots and lots. She would hear her most favourite music being played by her most favourite band. I'll go once, she thought; I'm not scared of Desraj.

On the way home from school on Friday Jamila invited Megan over for tea. 'My brother will be dropping something nice off to eat. You can come too, Luke, if you want.'

Luke and Megan both said they would ask if they were allowed.

'I have to go to a drum rehearsal first,' said Megan. 'Is that OK?'

Jamila and Luke looked at each other. 'Well, don't be too late,' said Jamila.

I have annoyed them both, thought Megan. What have I done wrong?

Megan called into the rehearsal on her way to Jamila's house. She remembered that very first time she had heard the Turbans. Then they were strangers playing strange sounds on instruments she had never seen before. Now, well she had even played with them.

Everyone but Desraj seemed pleased to see Megan. She sat on a chair in the corner and watched her favourite band play. Mr Singh seemed to be tough with the drummers tonight. He wasn't actually nasty, but he was very strict with them. He would have a sip of tea, and then shout, 'No! Do it again. That just wasn't good enough!'

In the five-minute break, Sanjit, the youngest of the group, explained why Mr Singh was being so hard. 'We are playing at a really big wedding in a few weeks' time. It is going to be filmed for TV as part of a documentary about Sikh people living in Wales. He just wants us to do our very best.'

After the break, Mr Singh made the group go over exactly what they had just played. Even Megan could tell there was some improvement. Mr Singh waited until the musicians had stopped and then said, 'What do you think, Megan?'

'Excellent,' she said. All the drummers but Desraj smiled at her. He just narrowed his eyes and gave her a horrible look.

Megan didn't stay until the end of the rehearsal because she didn't want to be late for tea at Jamila's. When she got there, Luke and Jamila were watching a film. They moved up the sofa to make room for her.

'Good rehearsal?' asked Luke.

'Brilliant,' said Megan.

'When are you going to play for us?' asked Jamila.

Soon, thought Megan, but not till I have my very own Mr Dhol.

It would be her birthday before long. There was only one thing she wanted, but she felt shy about asking for it. Then, one evening while the family sat around the dinner table, her mum said, 'What do you want for your birthday, love?'

'A drum,' said Megan without a second's hesitation.

'What kind?' asked her big brother, Martyn.

'An Indian one, stupid,' said Carys.

'There is more than one kind of Indian drum,' said Martyn in his I-know-more-about-music-than-you-do voice.

'A dhol drum. A bangra dhol drum,' said Megan.

Martyn didn't really know anything about Indian drums so he didn't know if she was making the words up or not.

'A Punjabi bangra dhol drum, please,' said Megan.

'I thought you hated musical instruments,' said Catrin.

'A dhol drum,' said Megan again. 'I don't want a new one. I want one that already knows how to play.'

Her brother and sisters laughed at her. A drum that already knows how to play? How foolish.

'I'll have a word with Mr Singh,' said Dad.

At the next Turbans' rehearsal Mr Singh asked Megan if she would like to come to the big wedding, the one that was going to be filmed. Desraj laughed and said, 'Why would she want to come to one of our parties?'

As Megan was leaving the youth club, Desraj caught up with her. He said, 'Look, I know Mr Singh is being kind, but the rest of us are sick of you. You don't fit in. Please don't come again.' Then he walked back into the club.

Somehow, thought Megan, I will go to that wedding. I want to see the greatest band in Wales play their most important gig ever. I want to hear magic at its very best.

Chapter 6

It was the week of the wedding. Five days until the filming. Mr Singh insisted that they rehearsed every night. Mr Singh seemed to be getting stricter and stricter with the band. They never answered back though. They knew that Mr Singh was on their side. They knew he would make them great.

Megan went to the rehearsal on Tuesday. The wedding was due to take place on Saturday. The Urban Turbans and Mr Singh were so busy that nobody spoke to Megan. Apart from nasty Desraj. He just whispered, 'Go and play with your toys, kid.'

On Wednesday evening Megan thought about going to the rehearsal. But the memory of Desraj's narrow eyes and nasty voice put her off. She stayed in her room most of the evening, playing Mr Dhol. She wondered if she would get a drum for her birthday. She hoped it would be as magical as Mr Dhol. She was afraid it might not be. How could it be? Mr Dhol had played a thousand times. Mr Dhol was wonderful. Wondrous. That was the word.

Megan decided to spend the rest of Wednesday

evening thinking about words that described her borrowed drum.

She didn't hear the knock at the front door; she had just decided that the drum was best described as sumptuous. She did hear Mum calling her name in an angry voice. When she heard this, it usually meant that her mum had been calling for some time.

Megan ran down the stairs to see what Mum wanted.

There in the hallway stood Mr Singh.

'Megan, take Mr Singh into the sitting room, please,' said Mum.

Mr Singh admired both pianos and then sat down by the fire. How strange, Megan thought, having the wonderful chief of drumming in her home. She rocked about on her feet a bit, and then sat down opposite Mr Singh. She put her hands in her lap, then she folded her arms. Next she put her hands on the chair arms. Mr Singh sat very still, smiling at her.

Megan thought she ought to 'make conversation' with Mr Singh but didn't know what to say. Just as she was about to try *Nice day, isn't it?* Mr Singh spoke.

'I suppose you are wondering why I am here,' he said.

'Yes. No. Yes. Don't know. Maybe. Well,' she said, suddenly remembering her manners, 'it is very nice of you to come.'

'I need to talk to you and your parents,' said Mr Singh.

It's Desraj, thought Megan. He has told Mr. Singh I'm rubbish. He has told Mr. Singh I am a waste of time.

The sitting room door opened and Megan's mother came in with a tray. She had made tea and had put out a plate of home-made Welsh cakes.

'Welsh cakes!' said Mr Singh. 'Just the thing to go with tea. I do like tea.' He took a Welsh cake and bit into it. 'You must give me the recipe,' he said. 'But first, I need to talk to you and Megan and your husband.'

'I am afraid my husband isn't here,' said Mum. 'He is out teaching.'

'Well, perhaps I can talk to you and you can talk to your husband afterwards. As you know, I run a drum group called the Urban Turbans . . .'

Megan's tummy jumped. She felt a prickly feeling at the back of her neck as if some creepy-crawly was creepily crawling across it. She touched her neck with her hand. Nothing there. Her face started to feel all hot. She wanted to run away.

'The group is playing on Saturday at a

wedding. It is going to be filmed for TV. The boys have been working very hard for it.'

Megan was trying to think of a good reason for leaving the room. She couldn't bear the thought of Mr Singh telling her mum that she was in the way and that the Urban Turbans thought that she was a silly little girl.

'I've got to go to the toilet!' she said quickly, and ran from the room. She locked herself in the bathroom. She stayed there for what seemed like hours but what was really only four and a half minutes. Surely by now Mr Singh would have gone?

He hadn't. When Megan slowly opened the sitting room door, she saw that Mum was pouring another cup of tea for Mr Singh. Both grown-ups turned and looked at her. They had a funny look on their faces. Not angry though.

'Megan!' said her mother in a rather loud voice. 'Go on, Mr Singh. Tell her!'

'I really need to ask her,' said Mr Singh. 'Megan, I need your help. Something has happened. Harpreet has fallen and broken his arm. He cannot play his drum. I . . . well we . . . wondered if you would do us the honour of playing with the Urban Turbans at the wedding on Saturday?'

THE HONOUR
THE HONOUR
HONOUR HONOUR
HON HON HONOUR

The words spun round in Megan's mind like the beat of a drum. After a few moments she heard Mum saying, 'Well, go on, Megan. Aren't you going to say yes?'

'Yes!' said Megan. 'Oh yes, please.'

Then she stopped and thought. No. No, it wasn't possible. She could hear Mr Singh saying she was the best junior drummer and that the wedding would be on quite late and . . . She couldn't do it. She was just a kid. Not even Indian. She certainly couldn't wear a turban.

'Megan!' said her mum.

Megan realised that she was crying. Her shoulders shook and big fat hot tears ran down both her cheeks.

Mr Singh said in a very quiet voice, 'What is the matter? I thought you would be pleased. You are excellent.'

Megan stood up. She said very slowly, 'I would love to. I feel, I feel honoured that you have asked me.' There, she'd tried out 'honoured' to see how it sounded. 'But . . . what would I wear?'

Megan's mum laughed. 'That's not a problem, cariad; we'll find you something.'

'Your favourite dress or trousers would be fine,' said Mr Singh.

'But . . .' said Megan

'Those trainers?' said Mr Singh.

'But . . .' How could she say it? That she would look silly, a Welsh girl playing Indian music with Indian boys.

'The boys will all be wearing blue, with bright blue turbans,' said Mr Singh.

'But I am not a boy and I am not a Sikh and I haven't got a turban!' Megan wailed.

'You don't have to be a boy to play the drum. You don't have to be Indian. You have a real feel for this music,' said Mr Singh. 'Besides, most of the Urban Turbans have never even been to India. They are Welsh Indian. Punjabi Indian. Punjabi Welsh. All sorts of people will be at the wedding. Besides, you don't need an Indian passport to be a good dhol player, Megan. As I say, there are all sorts of Welsh people . . .'

'Like us,' said Mum. 'I'm from Swansea, Dad's from Tenby and you and your brothers and sisters are Carmarthen Welsh!'

'Perhaps one day I could learn to play that harp,' said Mr Singh, looking across the room at

Catrin's. 'Or are only Welsh people allowed to play the harp? Next you will be saying that because I am from India, I am not allowed to make Welsh cakes!'

'I would be honoured to play with the Urban Turbans,' said Megan.

While Megan got ready, Mum quickly wrote down the Welsh cake recipe for Mr Singh.

There was no time to waste; the Urban Turbans were already down at the Youth Club, practising. As Megan and Mr Singh walked into the room, the Turbans began to clap. It was really funny because they started off clapping in the normal way, but then they started clapping to one of their drum rhythms.

'OK, folks,' said Mr Singh, 'it's time for some hard work.'

Megan put on her drum and looked at the drummers. Jagraj was smiling the most. She looked at Desraj, who smiled weakly. But at least he smiled.

Mr Singh counted them in, and off they went. There was no time to worry about it: Megan just had to let Mr Dhol do his stuff.

Chapter 7

Megan wore her favourite trousers and a sapphire-blue silk shirt. Mrs Singh, Mr Singh's wife, had given her a sparkly blue scarf from India which she wore bandana style, until she got too hot and had to take it off. She wore earrings borrowed from one sister and bangles from the other. On her feet she wore trainers, just like the rest of the band.

From a strong brown cord hung her drum. *Her* drum. The only one she could ever imagine playing at such an important event. As an early birthday present, Mum and Dad had bought it for Megan. There had been a large box on the table at breakfast time, tied with ribbon. Everybody had watched while she lifted off the layers of tissue paper, and they all laughed at her pink-cheeked pleasure as she exclaimed, 'Mr Dhol!'

This is how I want to be, thought Megan – a Welsh girl with an Indian drum, Mr Singh's best junior drummer. With my magical drum I can do this, play to a crowd of hundreds. Play well, she told herself, keep up with the Urban Turbans. On the one hand, Megan was brimming with confidence; on the other, she was afraid that she might let them down.

The wedding was being held in a huge room with long tables piled high with food. At one end there was a stage. Megan had been in the room for a rehearsal in the afternoon and had seen the arrival of huge delicious-smelling bowls and boxes. All her favourite food.

It was now seven o'clock in the evening and the TV cameras were already in place. Mr Singh was about to tell the wedding guests that the Urban Turbans would play for them.

Megan stood with the others outside the door to the wedding room. What if she played too slowly? What if she forgot what to do? What if Desraj had told people she was just a silly girl? She looked over at him. He was just putting his drum on when he suddenly looked up and smiled at her. She saw that he looked a bit worried too.

Jagraj spoke to the band. 'OK, guys, we are going to give them our very best. We will play for twenty minutes, that's all, but non-stop. After that we will have plenty of time for eating and enjoying ourselves. Good luck to all of us and special thanks to Megan for helping us out.'

Mr Singh climbed onto the stage. The wedding

guests stopped talking and eating long enough for him to say, 'And now, for your entertainment – the Urban Turbans and Megan!'

Jagraj pushed the doors open and the band entered the back of the room. They marched through to the stage, led by a small girl carrying a drum that looked almost as big as she was.

At one table sat Megan's family and, what a surprise, Luke and Jamila! They were smiling and clapping. As she walked past, they all whispered 'good luck' and Luke patted her arm. The whole room was clapping, pleased to see the band.

Megan's legs felt wobbly as she climbed up the stairs onto the stage. Her hands were shaking so badly, she wondered if she would be able to play. She looked up and saw a room full of smiling, friendly faces.

The drumming began. The band played and played and played. Megan's arms ached; her back ached. She felt bursts of light in her head, Indian light, like tiny little stars telling her to keep going. So she did. The band played loud and fast, everyone giving their best effort.

After twenty minutes of brilliant drumming, they stopped. People were whistling and shouting, clapping and banging on tables. Jagraj and the other Urban Turbans bowed and smiled.

Megan patted Mr Dhol. 'Thank you,' she whispered. She wasn't thanking the audience, or the band or even Mr Singh. She was talking to her drum. Her wonderful, magical, lovely drum. Hers to keep – forever!

Special Note

Sikhism is one of the world's major religions. It developed in India more than five hundred years ago. The word 'Sikh' comes from an ancient Indian language called Sanskrit. It means 'disciple' or 'learner'. Over a period of about two hundred and fifty years, ten special teachers called Gurus cared deeply for the ordinary people of India and showed them how to lead a good and holy life. Building on each other's work, the Gurus laid down important rules for the way people should live, such as respecting truth and love, working selflessly for others (whoever they are) and defending those who are weak.

Sikhs believe in one God, and worship in a Gurdwara. Although prayers can be offered to God anywhere and at any time, the Gurdwara is a place where people can gather to worship together. Although some Gurdwaras can be very elaborate, they can be as simple as a temporary shack or a small room in a house.

Today Sikhs may be found all over the world and there are about 600,000 Sikhs in Britain, mostly in urban or city areas. They observe special rules called the five Ks.

Kesh is the first K: it means uncut hair (a gift from God), which is why many Sikhs, both men and women, wear a turban (sometimes called a *dastaar*). The other four Ks all involve wearing something special: Kanga (a wooden comb); Kara (a bracelet); Kaccha (a cotton undergarment) and Kirpan (a small decorative sword). If you would like to find out more about the five Ks, or anything else about the Sikh faith, you will find the following website very helpful:

http://atschool.eduweb.co.uk/carolrb/sikhism/sikhism1.html

MEET THE AUTHOR

Can a Welsh girl be an Indian drummer?

That's what Megan has to find out in *The Urban Turbans*, Dahlian Kirby's first novel for children. It highlights her special interest in the way different cultures overlap – in real life as well as in fiction. Originally from the north-east of England, Dahlian settled in Wales many years ago and works as both a teacher and writer. She is enthusiastic about Indian drumming and likes stories about 'brave girls'. Dahlian lives with her husband, pets and drums in the Vale of Glamorgan.